I Remember

written by Jeanne Willis

illustrated by Raquel Catalina

nosy crow

There was someone at Kathleen's door.
It was a little boy in a blue coat.

"How lovely to see you!" said Kathleen.
"Come in."

The boy came in and made himself
at home.

"I haven't seen you for a while," said Kathleen.
"Not since yesterday," he said.
"Was it only yesterday?" she wondered.
"Yes," said the boy, "but it feels like forever,
because I missed you and you missed me.
We had so much fun, didn't we?"
"Remind me," said Kathleen . . .

"Well, first I gave you a cuddle," he said, "then you cuddled me back."

"Like this?" asked Kathleen.

"Just like that," said the boy. "Then you gave me a chocolate biscuit."

"Did I?" said Kathleen.

"Yes, because they're my favourite – are there any more?"

"I can't remember where I put them," said Kathleen.

"I can," said the boy.

"I'm good at finding biscuits."

There was only one left . . .

so he broke it in half, and they shared it.

"What day is it?" asked Kathleen.
"What time is it?"
"It's today," said the boy, "and it's time to play in the garden."
"Is it?" said Kathleen.
"Yes," he said. "Put your blue coat on, then we will look like twins."

But Kathleen's buttons wouldn't behave . . .

no matter how hard . . .   she tried.

She got upset, but the boy understood perfectly.
"Buttons are fiddly," he said, "but I can do them up all by myself
now I'm five — I'll show you if you don't believe me."
He did Kathleen's buttons up and looked very pleased with himself.

"You are clever!" said Kathleen. "I wish I was your age. It's odd — I can remember being five, but I can't remember what I did five minutes ago."
"I expect that's because it was boring," said the boy.

Kathleen followed him into the garden.

"Let's play," he said. "This bench is your spaceship."
"Who am I?" said Kathleen.
"An astronaut," said the boy. "I'm the pilot, and the pigeons are invading aliens. I'll climb up the tree, then leap out and rescue you, okay?"

He climbed up the rope swing

and stood high in the tree . . .

whilst Kathleen sat in the spaceship.

After a few moments, Kathleen began to worry.
"Help! Help! Where am I?"

"Do not be afraid!" said the boy.
"I have come to rescue you from the
aliens. Whoosh — boom — shoo!

You're safe now," he said.
"I will take you back to Planet Earth."
He steered Kathleen back indoors . . .

. . . and helped her into the armchair.

"Well, that was quite an adventure, Joe!" she laughed.

"I'm George," he said.

"George? I've got a grandson called George," said Kathleen.

"You remind me of him very much."

"What is he like?" asked the boy.

"He's the best boy in the world," said Kathleen.

"He has a blue coat just like yours — he can do the buttons up all by himself, you know?"

"Yes, I do know," he said.

"Really? Have you met my George?" asked Kathleen.

"I am your George,"
said the boy.

He fetched the photo that she
kept on the mantelpiece.

"That's you . . . and that's me,"
he said, "when we were younger."

"How could I forget my own grandson's name?" she sighed.
George tucked a flower behind her ear.
"Don't cry, Grandma," he said.
"I'll always be here to remind you."

"You remembered I'm the best boy in the world – that's all that matters to me. Shall we dance? Dancing makes you happy."

"What if I fall?" said Grandma.

"I'll catch you," said George. "I catched a ginormous elephant once – all by myself!"

"You **caught** a ginormous elephant," corrected Grandma.

"Yes, I did," said George. "And if I caught an elephant, I can catch you."

"I haven't got any dance music,"
she said.
"Sing that song you sang to me when
I was a baby – we can dance to that,"
said George, and he started to hum it.

"'Mr Sandman'? I remember that
one!" said Grandma.

She sang,

and they danced

and danced

until . . .

. . . they both ran out of puff.

"You're a very good dancer," said George.

"And you're a very good boy, Joe," said Grandma.

She'd forgotten his name again, but George didn't mind a bit.

"You love me whoever I am, don't you?"
he smiled.
"More than words can say," she said,
"and don't you forget it!"

"I won't," he promised.
Because George knew that even if
Grandma's mind forgot who he was . . .

. . . her heart always remembered.